Dina the Rapper

Level 3H

Written by Lucy George
Illustrated by Andrew Geeson

What is synthetic phonics?

Synthetic phonics teaches children to recognise the sounds of letters and to blend (synthesise) them together to make whole words.

Understanding sound/letter relationships gives children the confidence and ability to read unfamiliar words, without having to rely on memory or guesswork; this helps them progress towards independent reading.

Did you know? Spoken English uses more than 40 speech sounds. Each sound is called a *phoneme*. Some phonemes relate to a single letter (d-o-g) and others to combinations of letters (sh-ar-p). When a phoneme is written down it is called a *grapheme*. Teaching these sounds, matching them to their written form and sounding out words for reading is the basis of synthetic phonics.

Consultant

I love reading phonics has been created in consultation with language expert Abigail Steel. She has a background in teaching and teacher training and is a respected expert in the field of Synthetic Phonics. Abigail Steel is a regular contributor to educational publications. Her international education consultancy supports parents and teachers in the promotion of literacy skills.

Reading tips

This book focuses on the sound:
er as in 'rapper'

Tricky words in this book

Any words in bold may have unusual spellings or are new and have not yet been introduced.

Tricky words in this book:

worked diner wanted when busy there zipped their came gave counter jukebox finer ate

Extra ways to have fun with this book

- After the reader has read the story, ask them questions about what they have just read:

What did Dina want to be at the start of the story?
What did Dina give T-Rex to eat when he came in to the diner?

- Make flashcards of the focus graphemes. Ask the reader to say the sounds. This will help reinforce letter/sound matches.

A pronunciation guide

This grid contains the sounds used in the story and a guide on how to say them.

s as in sat	a as in ant	t as in tin	p as in pig	i as in ink
n as in net	c as in cat	e as in egg	h as in hen	r as in rat
m as in mug	d as in dog	g as in get	o as in ox	u as in up
l as in log	f as in fan	b as in bag	j as in jug	v as in van
w as in wet	z as in zip	y as in yet	k as in kit	qu as in quick
x as in box	ff as in off	ll as in ball	ss as in kiss	zz as in buzz
ck as in duck	pp as in puppy	nn as in bunny	rr as in arrow	gg as in egg
dd as in daddy	bb as in chubby	tt as in attic	sh as in shop	ch as in chip
th as in them	th as in the	ng as in sing	nk as in sunk	le as in bottle
ai as in rain	ee as in feet	ie as in pies	oa as in oak	ue as in cue
ar as in park	er as in term	er as in mixer		

Be careful not to add an 'uh' sound to 's', 't', 'p', 'c', 'h', 'r', 'm', 'd', 'g', 'l', 'f' and 'b'. For example, say 'fff' not 'fuh' and 'sss' not 'suh'.

Dina **worked** in the **diner**.

She **wanted** to be a rapper.

When it was **busy**,

she worked harder.

"Waiter! **There** is no butter!"

Dina **zipped** to get butter for **their** table.

“Waiter! **Chowder**!”

Dina was quick to bring it.

Dina wanted to be a rapper,

but did not fuss.

One day T-Rex **came** to the diner.

T-Rex was a rapper!

Dina was so happy! “Yes!”

Dina **gave** T-Rex a very big burger.

And a free beef and herb pie.

And extra fries.

And a jug of fizzy drink!

But T-Rex just **ate** his burger up.

He did not see Dina.

T-Rex put on his coat! He was off!

It was Dina's cue... her only shot!

Think!

Dina put on the **jukebox** and got on the counter.

She went, 'I'm rapping in my diner!

There's nothing else that's **finer**!'

T-Rex loved Dina's rap. Now Dina and T-Rex are both rappers at the diner!

OVER 48 TITLES IN SIX LEVELS

Abigail Steel recommends...

Other titles to enjoy from Level 3

978-1-84898-552-0

978-1-84898-398-4

978-1-84898-399-1

Some titles from Level 1

978-1-84898-277-2

978-1-84898-396-0

978-1-84898-548-3

978-1-84898-547-6

Some titles from Level 2

978-1-84898-386-1

978-1-84898-387-8

978-1-84898-550-6

978-1-84898-549-0

An Hachette UK Company
www.hachette.co.uk

First published in Great Britain in 2012 by TickTock, a division of Octopus Publishing Group Ltd,
Endeavour House, 189 Shaftesbury Avenue, London WC2H 8JY.
www.octopusbooks.co.uk

ISBN 978 1 84898 558 2

Printed and bound in China
10 9 8 7 6 5 4 3 2 1